First published 2012 by Macmillan Children's Books, a division of Macmillan Publishers Limited, 20 New Wharf Road, London N1 9RR Basingstoke and Oxford Associated companies throughout the world www.panmacmillan.com

ISBN: 978-0-230-75440-9 (HB)
ISBN: 978-0-230-75441-6 (PB)
Text and illustrations copyright © Rebecca Patterson 2012
Moral rights asserted.

1 3 5 7 9 8 6 4 2

A CIP catalogue record for this book is available from the British Library.

Printed in China

To the children
in Akeman Street
R.P.

The Pirate House

Rebecca Patterson

MACMILLAN CHILDREN'S BOOKS

No one knew who lived in that house on the corner. But when all those seagulls flew onto the roof, Sam Turner said it must be . . .

PIRATES!

And we knew it WAS pirates when we saw the tide had gone out of their pond and there was a shell and some GOLD left in the bottom!

We never looked at the pirate washing.

If you did you turned into a jellyfish.

Even on a sunny day we could hear the wind howling inside the pirate house.

And someone said that once a fish
fell out of the letterbox.

The postman had to post it back.

Sam Turner says that at night the sea fills the house and it GLOWS like an aquarium.

But the pirates never come out. They are
busy having parties for baby mermaids . . .

... and counting their gold.

Last Thursday, the front door of the pirate house started to open . . .

Sam Turner shouted, "HOLD YOUR BREATH!
A HUGE WAVE WILL COME OUT!"

So we all held our breath.

The door opened wider . . . and wider . . .

But it wasn't a wave that came out.
Or a pirate. It was . . .

. . . a **LADY**, and she told us
to stop leaning on her fence.

We said to Sam Turner, "That's **NOT** a pirate!"
And we all went home for our teas.

The next day Sam Turner ran
up shouting, "GUESS WHAT? There are
MONSTERS moving into Number 2!"

We laughed and said to Sam Turner,

". . . nothing EVER happens on our street!"